Never Ever Talk to Strangers!

by Anne Marie Pace
Illustrated by Guy Francis

Scholastic Inc.
New York   Toronto   London   Auckland
Sydney   Mexico City   New Delhi   Hong Kong

To my four bears and their Papa Bear
—A.M.P.

For my daughter Sammie
—G.F.

ISBN 978-0-545-24229-5

12 11 10 9 8 7 6 5 4 3 2 1   10 11 12 13 14 15/0

Printed in the U.S.A.   40
First printing, September 2010

Climbing down the school bus steps, Jamie opened his jacket so Mom would see the shiny badge Officer Crane had pinned to Jamie's shirt during the school assembly.

"Super Safety Expert," Mom read. "Congratulations!"

While he ate his snack, Jamie told Mom all the
rules Officer Crane had taught them.

"Strangers are people you don't know. If a stranger talks to you, you should yell and run away. And Mrs. Otter hung my 'Never Talk to Strangers' poster on the wall!" he said.

Later, Mom needed to clean the garage, so Jamie went to the backyard to kick his soccer ball.

THWACK! Jamie's first kick sent the ball bouncing into the net.

THWACK! So did his second.

THWACK! His third ball soared over the net.
It landed in the yard of the empty house next door.
Jamie slipped through a gap in the fence to retrieve it.

"Looking for this?" a voice said.
Jamie jumped. No one had lived in that house
since the Wolf family moved. But someone Jamie
had never seen before was holding the soccer ball.

"Thanks," Jamie said. Stretching out his hand for the ball, Jamie took a couple of steps forward.

But then the late afternoon sunlight glinted off
Jamie's chest and he remembered his shiny badge.
His tummy started to do flips. Who was this person?
And what was he doing in the Wolfs' backyard?

Jamie froze. This was a stranger.
What had Officer Crane said to do about strangers?

"You're a stranger!" Jamie yelled as he dashed back through the fence. "Mom! MOOOOOOOM!" He ran toward his back porch and leaped up the steps. Inside, he slammed the door and turned the lock.

He leaned against the door, his heart pounding.

Mom rushed into the kitchen. "Jamie!" she cried. "I heard you yelling."

Seeing Mom made him feel safer. "I talked to a stranger," he told her. "Then I got really scared."

Mom hugged him. "Everything's fine now, buddy," she said. "You're safe."

Jamie looked down at his badge. "But I'm not a Super Safety Expert. I broke Officer Crane's number one rule—never talk to strangers."

The doorbell rang. "Hold on, Jamie," Mom said.
"We'll talk more in a minute."

Mom stood up and walked to the front hall. Jamie
unpinned his badge and stuffed it in his pocket. He
didn't want to wear it anymore.

"Mr. Fox!" Mom said. Her voice sounded cheerful. "How good to see you!"

Jamie peeked out around the corner. It was the man from next door. Why was Mom letting the stranger into the house? And why was Mom smiling at him?

"I've unpacked and I wanted to say hello," Mr. Fox said. "And I brought this ball back."

Jamie ran into the hall and tugged Mom's skirt, pulling her ear down to his mouth. "Mom, that's the stranger. Don't let him in. Never talk to strangers!"

For a moment, Mom looked confused. "Mr. Fox isn't a stranger. He was my piano teacher when—"

Suddenly, Mom paused, nodding in understanding.
"I see what you mean, Jamie. I've known Mr. Fox since
I was a little girl, but of course, he is a stranger to *you*."

Mr. Fox stretched out his hand. "I'm sorry I scared you, Jamie," Mr. Fox said as they shook hands.

"I shouldn't have talked to you," Jamie said. "I didn't know you yet."

Mom knelt beside Jamie. "You did talk to a
stranger, Jamie, and I can see why you were upset.
But let's talk about the things you did right."

Jamie thought, then began counting on his fingers. "When I realized he was a stranger, I stopped walking toward him. Then I shouted that I didn't know him and I yelled for a parent."

He touched his third finger. "And then I ran away as fast as I could, got inside, and locked the door."

Mom squeezed Jamie's hand. "It sounds to me
like you *are* a Super Safety Expert."

"You did exactly the right things, Jamie," Mr. Fox said. "I hope we can be friends, now that your mom has told you it's okay."

"Why don't you show Mr. Fox your badge?" Mom said.

Jamie slowly pulled the badge out from his pocket
and handed it to Mr. Fox.

Mr. Fox turned it around and admired it. "This is a
mighty fine badge. May I?" Jamie nodded and Mr. Fox
pinned the badge back on Jamie's shirt.

"I happen to have a delicious apple pie next door," said Mr. Fox. "Now that we're friends, would you and your mom like to come over for tea?"

Smiling, Jamie nodded. It was good to have a new friend, it was even better to know he had done the right things, and it was awesome knowing that he was a Super Safety Expert, after all.

OFFICER CRANE SAYS . . .

A stranger is someone you don't know. Most strangers are nice, but a few of them are not. Because you cannot tell who is nice and who is not by looking, it is very, very important to let your parents (or the grown-ups who take care of you) tell you whether or not it is okay to talk to someone you have never met before.

OFFICER CRANE'S RULES FOR STRANGER SAFETY

1. Always stay with your parents or babysitter. If they give you permission to be somewhere alone (your backyard, for example), stay there.

2. If a stranger approaches you, back away. If the stranger comes closer, run away and yell, "I don't know you. You're a stranger," just like Jamie did.

3. Never go anywhere with a stranger. Sometimes strangers might offer you treats or ask you for help. You shouldn't take anything from a stranger. And if a stranger asks you for help finding a lost pet or a certain house in your neighborhood, don't do it. Adults should ask other adults to help them.

4. You might have to talk to a stranger if you get lost in a busy place, like a grocery store or the mall. Stop walking and look for a mommy with kids or a person who works in the store behind the cash register. Tell that person that you are lost and you need help. That person can help you find a police officer or your parents.

5. Talk to your parents about what to say when you answer the phone. When someone you don't know calls, put your parents on the phone or talk to the caller using the words your parents have taught you to say. If you get an email from a stranger, tell your parents right away.